"I DON'T LIKE ̶̶̶̶̶̶OUR OWN ADVENTURE̶̶̶̶̶OKS. I *LOVE* THEM!" says Jessica Gordon, age 10. And now, kids between the ages of six and nine can choose their own adventure, too. Here's what kids have to say about the Skylark Choose Your Own Adventure® books.

"These are my favorite books because you can pick whatever choice you want—and the story is all about you."
—**Katy Alson,** *age 8*

"I love finding out how my story will end."
—**Joss Williams,** *age 9*

"I like all the illustrations!"
—**Savitri Brightfield,** *age 7*

"A six-year-old friend and I have lots of fun making the decisions together."
—**Peggy Marcus** *(adult)*

Bantam Skylark Books in the Choose Your Own
    Adventure® Series
Ask your bookseller for the books you have missed

# JUNGLE SAFARI

## EDWARD PACKARD

# ILLUSTRATED BY LORNA TOMEI

A BANTAM SKYLARK BOOK®
TORONTO · NEW YORK · LONDON · SYDNEY

RL 2, 007–009

JUNGLE SAFARI

*A Bantam Skylark Book / November 1983*

*CHOOSE YOUR OWN ADVENTURE® is a registered trademark of Bantam Books, Inc.*

*Original Conception of Edward Packard*
*Front cover art by Paul Granger*

*Skylark Books is a registered trademark of Bantam Books, Inc.*
*Registered in U.S. Patent and Trademark Office and elsewhere.*

ISBN 0-553-15226-2

*Published simultaneously in the United States and Canada*

---

*Bantam Books are published by Bantam Books, Inc. Its trademark, consisting of the words "Bantam Books" and the portrayal of a rooster, is Registered in U.S. Patent and Trademark Office and in other countries. Marca Registrada. Bantam Books, Inc., 666 Fifth Avenue, New York, New York 10103.*

---

PRINTED IN THE UNITED STATES OF AMERICA

CW      0 9 8 7 6 5 4 3 2 1

# JUNGLE SAFARI

# NARUBI JUNGLE

DAKARA Hills

TRAIL

Falls

MAKATAN VILLAGE

N W E S

RAPIDS

BANTA RIVER

# READ THIS FIRST!!!

Most books are about other people.

This book is about *you* and your adventures on a jungle safari.

Do not read this book from the first page through to the last page. Instead, start on page one and read until you come to your first choice. Then turn to the page shown and see what happens.

When you come to the end of a story, you can go back and start again. Every choice leads to a new adventure.

Good luck, and watch out for lions, elephants, snakes, gorillas, termites, scorpions . . . and rhinoceroses!

Your uncle Stanley is a game warden, and **1** his daughter, June, is your favorite cousin. They've asked you to go with them on a jungle safari. You'll have a chance to see wild animals running free. Maybe you'll even see the Kawamba, a great ape that once lived in the Dakara Hills.

Uncle Stanley thinks that a few Kawambas may still be alive—somewhere in the thickest part of the jungle. Though no one has seen a Kawamba in many, many years, some people say they have heard its call—a long, low whistle that sounds like a flute.

Are you ready to go? Then make a list of what to bring and load up your pack. . . .

*Turn to page 2.*

**2**    You've spent the first day of the safari in Uncle Stanley's Land Rover, bumping along dirt tracks to the edge of the Narubi Jungle. Now it's the darkest time of night. You're lying on a cot in your tent. June is sleeping quietly nearby. A pale moon is shining. You can hear the cries and calls of animals outside.

Uncle Stanley is sleeping in another tent. You wish he were here, because there's something that scares you. It may be nothing, you tell yourself.

At last you fall asleep. You dream of monkeys and hippos and giraffes. When you open your eyes, it's daylight.

*Go on to the next page.*

*HSSSS!* Something is slithering over your legs. *HSSSSS!* It's one of the most deadly snakes in the world—the green mamba!

*If you try to grab the snake by the neck so it can't move its head, turn to page 44.*

*If you try to roll away from the snake, turn to page 9.*

*If you lie perfectly still, turn to page 20.*

**4**    Uncle Stanley blows up the raft. You and June get your packs and climb aboard.

"I think we'll reach the Dakara Hills about twelve miles downstream," says Stanley. "We should be there in a few hours if all goes well."

As the raft drifts downstream, you see

flamingos grouped in the shallows. A pygmy **5**
hippo stares at you from the shore. A croco-
dile swims past but doesn't seem to see you.

---

*Go on to page 6.*

**6** "What's that noise up ahead?" you ask.

"Rapids," Stanley answers. "They sound bad, but we can't turn back. Get ready—it's going to be rough."

Soon the raft is swept into raging white waters. Stanley paddles on one side, and you and June on the other. Heavy white spray flies in your face. The raft tilts, and you and June are thrown into the swirling waters.

*Turn to page 16.*

**8**    The morning air is fresh and cool. The scary sounds of the night are gone. You can hear doves cooing. Quickly you get dressed and load your pack for the day ahead.

Uncle Stanley spreads a map before you. "From here we go into the Narubi Jungle on foot. If we take this trail, we should reach the Dakara Hills by nightfall. That's where the Kawambas were last seen."

"But isn't that trail used by lions and leopards?" June asks. "Let's inflate the raft and go down the Banta River until we reach the Dakara Hills."

"That might be wise," says Uncle Stanley, "but we don't know what the river is like." He turns to you. "Are you willing to risk going through the rapids?"

*If you say you'd rather follow the jungle trail, turn to page 14.*

*If you say you'd rather raft down the river, turn to page 4.*

Like a flash you roll out of bed—so fast **9** you crash right into June's cot.

"SNAKE! SNAKE!" June yells. She points at the mamba, which is racing across the floor. Uncle Stanley runs into the tent and prods the snake with the butt of his gun. The mamba wiggles out of the tent. *Phew!*

"Someone didn't zip up the tent flap," says Stanley, sternly. He pokes around to make sure there are no other snakes in the tent. "I'm sure everyone will be more careful from now on."

"Dad sounded angry," June says after your uncle leaves, "but he's worried about us and this safari. Many people have gone into the Narubi Jungle and have never been seen again."

*Turn to page 8.*

**10**   You run down the path but then stop. You're *not* alone. Beyond the tangle of vines, eyes are watching.

A trumpet blast pierces your ears! Out of the forest comes a huge elephant, its ears and trunk waving. Its fierce eyes are looking right at you! You have to think fast. Should you try to hide, or should you run?

*If you hide behind a tree, turn to page 21.*

*If you run, turn to page 15.*

**12**     You climb up on the termite mound. It seems as hard as a rock. Those termites build strong houses!

From the top of the mound you can see a path leading up a high hill. You drink some water from your canteen, climb down from the mound, and start walking.

After a three-hour trek, you reach a stream. You're hot and tired, so you splash water on your face to cool off. Then, as you look around, you notice a family of gorillas. They're only a few dozen yards away. They are crouched near the water, eating wild celery.

A big gorilla with silver hair on his back rears up. He stares at you, beats his enormous chest, and lets out a loud roar.

As you stand there, trembling with fear, a smaller gorilla looks at you and shakes its head from side to side.

*Go on to the next page.*

If you turn and run, turn to page 24.

If you shake your head and try to act like a gorilla, turn to page 26.

If you try to wade across the stream, turn to page 38.

"I'm glad we decided to follow the jungle trail," says Uncle Stanley as you tramp through the brush. "We may see an okapi—they're related to giraffes—or even a gorilla."

"I hope we don't see any leopards," says June.

You walk through the hot, steamy jungle for hours. Two brightly colored parrots chase each other through the trees, and you stop to watch them. Soon they're out of sight—and so are June and Uncle Stanley! They've gone on ahead, and you're all alone.

*Turn to page 10.*

You run from the elephant, racing through **15** a thicket so fast the thorns rip your shirt and scratch your arm. The elephant mows down bushes and small trees as it chases you. You dart to one side and climb a tree. Looking over the bushes, you see the elephant waving its trunk angrily.

Suddenly it lumbers off through the brush.

You slide to the ground. If you can find your way back to the river, you can follow it downstream and maybe find June and Uncle Stanley, or perhaps a friendly village.

*Turn to page 22.*

**16**     The river sweeps you downstream. It's hard to keep your head above water. Then you see a big log floating nearby. You grab hold, just as something tugs on your leg. It's June!

"Hang on tight!" she screams. But you can't hang on. You, June, and the log shoot over the falls and plunge down deep into the swirling water.

At last you bob to the surface.

June is clinging to the log, just a few feet away. "Are you okay?" she yells over the roar of the falls.

*Turn to page 19.*

**18**     You keep walking along the trail. It's hot and muggy in the trees. You're happy when you reach open land and feel a cool breeze on your face.

Ahead of you is a plain, but the grass is so tall you can't see very far. You *can* see a termite mound that's about four feet tall. If you climbed on top of it, you could see over the grass and figure out which way to go. But suppose the mound gave way? You might fall into a nest of thousands of angry termites!

*If you decide to climb up on the termite mound, turn to page 12.*

*If you decide to keep walking through the tall grass, turn to page 42.*

"I think so." You swim to the log and hold **19** on while you catch your breath.

"We've got to get back to my father," June says. "I think we can steer this log to shore by paddling with our hands. But maybe we should just ride it downstream. We might reach a village where we could get help."

*If you decide to ride the log downstream, turn to page 28.*

*If you decide to paddle to shore, turn to page 34.*

**20**   You lie perfectly still. A moment later the snake slides off your leg and flops onto the floor.

"June, wake up!" You jump out of bed and poke the snake with a shovel, pushing it outdoors. Then you zip the tent flap shut.

June is sitting up on her cot—wide-eyed. "You sure did the right thing!"

You're shaking too much to answer.

"As my dad says," June adds, "when you're in the jungle, you've got to think fast."

*Turn to page 8.*

You run behind a tree, then shrink back as **21** the elephant wraps his trunk around it. He shakes the tree like a stick. Leaves and twigs tumble down. You'd better make a break for it!

You dart and weave through the brush, then dive into a dense thicket and keep very still. The elephant charges past like an express train! You wait a few minutes, then crawl out of the thicket and start back along the trail. But soon you know that you are lost.

*Turn to page 18.*

**22**   You keep walking toward the river. You find an animal trail and follow it, thinking that it may connect with the trail where you last saw June and Uncle Stanley. You haven't gone very far when your way is blocked by a rock wall. Through the tall grass you can see a small opening in the wall. Could it be the entrance to a cave?

Suddenly you hear a noise behind you. You turn to look. A rhinoceros is walking slowly toward you.

*If you crawl into the opening in the rock wall, turn to page 27.*

*If you run through the tall grass and into the forest, turn to page 39.*

**24**    You turn to run. The big gorilla charges! You duck, but the gorilla swings, hits you in the seat of your pants, and sends you flying through the air. You are knocked out cold.

When you wake up, a smaller gorilla is near you. Out of the corner of your eye you can see the big one nearby.

The small gorilla shoves a stalk of wild celery into your mouth. You don't really want it, but you eat a bite, because you realize that you've been accepted into the gorilla family.

During the days ahead, you live with the band of gorillas. They feed you fruits and wild vegetables. Soon you learn to gather them yourself. You sleep in trees and play with the young gorillas. Your food is raw and tastes bitter, but you grow lean and tough as a wild animal.

*Turn to page 49.*

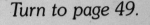

**26**   You grab some wild celery and stuff it in your mouth. While you chew on the bitter stalk, you shake your head, copying the young gorilla.

After a few moments, the big gorilla stops pounding his chest and sits down. Maybe as long as you can act like a baby gorilla, you'll be safe.

*Turn to page 36.*

You crawl into the opening. You're in a **27** tunnel. It gets narrower. You're afraid you'll get stuck. Then it gets wider. Luckily, you brought your flashlight. You shine it all around and see that you have reached a small cave.

The walls are wet and slimy. Water drips from the ceiling. A few feet away is a pile of bones and skulls.

You've had enough of this cave! You start back toward the entrance, but now your path is blocked by a scary crawling creature. It's a scorpion. And it might be poisonous.

*Turn to page 31.*

**28**   You and June hold onto the log and let the current take you downstream. Soon you hear a roaring sound up ahead. "What's that noise?" you yell at June. "It sounds like another waterfall!"

"It's another waterfall, all right!" June yells. "Only *bigger!*"

As you drift helplessly downstream, the roar of the waterfall grows louder. Will it be like the last one?

Oh, no! This waterfall is much, much, much higher.

**The End**

**30**    You run and find June and Uncle Stanley. "I'm sure I heard the whistle of the Kawamba," you tell them.

"Quick, lead us to it!" Stanley says.

The three of you hike for hours through the dense forest. Just once, you all hear the whistle again, but you never catch sight of the strange animal.

"There is no doubt that the whistle we heard was the call of the Kawamba," Stanley says, as you head back along the trail toward home.

"Just *hearing* it made the trip worthwhile," says June. "Well . . . *almost* worthwhile."

"Someday I'll come back," you say. "Someday I'll find the Kawamba."

### The End

You pick up the longest bone and use it to **31** shoo away the scorpion as you crawl back through the tunnel. *Phew!* You made it outside, and the rhinoceros is gone!

You hurry along the trail. What's that sound? Drums. There must be a village nearby. You hurry toward the sound, jogging through groves of tamarind trees. Finally you reach a tiny village. June and Uncle Stanley are there!

---

*Go on to the next page.*

**32**  "We've been searching for you all day," Stanley says. "The villagers hoped you would hear their drums."

"Well, I did, and look at this—from a cave full of bones!" You hold out the bone you've been carrying all the way from the cave.

Stanley takes the bone and looks at it closely. "If I'm not mistaken," he says, "you have found the burial cave of the Kawambas. Even if none of them are alive today, scientists will study their bones, and we can learn how they looked and how they lived."

**The End**

**34**    You and June paddle the log toward shore. At last you reach the grassy bank.

"A boy is standing there. "Jambo, hello," he says, smiling. "You are as wet as a fish."

"And colder than a fish," June says with a shiver.

"If you come with me to Makatan Village, there will be a fire and food."

You and June follow the boy to a small hut with a grass roof. His mother, Koka, gives you rice and fruit, and tells you that the villagers have gone to rescue Uncle Stanley. She asks you to spend the night in the village.

That night Koka tells the stories of Sungura, the clever hare who tricks all the jungle animals.

When Uncle Stanley joins you, you know your jungle safari is over. All your supplies were swept away in the rapids. You never found the Kawambas, but you did find some very good friends.

**The End**

**36**     That afternoon, when the gorillas are taking a nap, you sneak away. As you follow a trail away from the stream, you hear something crashing through the brush—coming straight at you! You dive under a bush. The noise comes closer. It's June and Uncle Stanley!

"Thank goodness we found you," says **37**
Uncle Stanley. "From now on *let's stay together!*"

## The End

**38**    You walk into the stream. The big gorilla follows. He stops at the bank and lets out a roar so loud it hurts your ears. You shake with fear as you hurry across, but you can tell that the gorilla doesn't want to get wet.

For the moment you're safe. You reach the other side of the stream, climb out, and start walking downhill.

*Turn to page 22.*

You run through the tall grass, along the **39** rock wall and into the forest. It's not long before you reach the river. As you start walking along its bank, you hear a loud bellow from up ahead.

*Turn to page 47.*

Then you hear another whistle—this one from deep within the woods. The Kawamba vanishes into the brush so quickly you almost wonder if you saw it at all!

You hurry back past the battling hippos and finally reach June and Uncle Stanley. They are amazed when you tell them about the Kawamba, and the three of you begin a search.

Unfortunately, you never see or hear the Kawamba again, and when you return home, nobody believes your story—unless you took a picture, of course.

**The End**

**42**     You keep walking through the tall grass. But you can't be sure you're headed the right way. What's worse, you hear a funny noise in the grass behind you. What could it be?

You walk faster. But the thing behind you moves faster, too.

You start to run. But the thing behind you is running, too.

You're afraid to look around, and with good reason!

## The End

**44**    You try to grab the snake by the neck so it can't move its head. It strikes at your arm. You pull away, but the mamba is too fast.

OWWWOUCH!

Uncle Stanley runs into your tent. He pushes the snake outside with his gun.

"Oh, no." He looks closely at your arm. "A mamba bite is serious. We'll have to get you back to the clinic right away—they'll give you a shot. You'll be okay, but it's going to hurt."

A few minutes later you, June, and Uncle Stanley are back in the Land Rover bouncing along the dirt tracks.

Your jungle safari is over.

**The End**

If only you could hear the whistle again, **45**
you could tell where it was coming from.
Then you hear it—directly overhead! Something drops from the trees—an ape covered
with curly orange-red hair and a face that
looks almost human. It's a Kawamba. Staring
right at you!

*Did you bring a camera? If you did, you
quickly take a picture!*

*Turn to page 41.*

Through a clearing in the brush, you see **47** two giant hippos battling each other like army tanks! Partly in the river, partly out, they thrash around, sending sheets of water flying in all directions.

---

*Go on to the next page.*

**48**     Then you see Stanley and June further downstream! They have stopped to watch the hippos but haven't seen you. You don't dare walk toward them; you'd be too close to the battling hippos. So you start through the brush, hoping to reach them quickly. Then you hear a long, low whistle that sounds like a flute. It seems to have come from high in a tree, no more than a hundred feet away.

*If you walk toward where the whistle came from, turn to page 45.*

*If you try to get back to the others as quickly as possible, turn to page 30.*

A month later a team of scientists finds **49** you. They have come to the jungle to learn more about gorillas. They are eager to hear about your adventures with the gorillas, for you have learned more about these wonderful animals than almost anyone else in the world.

*Go on to the next page.*

**50**    A few days later you are back with June and Uncle Stanley.

"It's great to see you again," June says.

"It sure is," Uncle Stanley adds. "I hope

you'll come with us again. Next time we'll **51**
find the Kawamba!"

## **The End**

## ABOUT THE AUTHOR

**Edward Packard,** a graduate of Princeton University and Columbia Law School, practiced law in New York and Connecticut before turning to writing full time. He developed the unique storytelling approach used in the Choose Your Own Adventure® series while thinking up stories for his children, Caroline, Andrea, and Wells.

## ABOUT THE ILLUSTRATOR

**Lorna Tomei** studied painting and illustration at the Art Students League and the School of Visual Arts in New York. She has illustrated more than a dozen children's books, including *Help! You're Shrinking* and *Dream Trips* in the Bantam Skylark Choose Your Own Adventure® series, and is a frequent contributor to children's magazines. Ms. Tomei lives in Centerport, Long Island, with her husband, two sons, one dog, three rats, two cats, and a very crabby parrot.

# DO YOU LOVE
# CHOOSE YOUR OWN ADVENTURE®?
# Let your older brothers and sisters in on the fun.

You know how great CHOOSE YOUR OWN AD-VENTURE® books are to read over and over again. But did you know that there are CHOOSE YOUR OWN ADVENTURE® books for older kids too? They're just as much fun as the CHOOSE YOUR OWN AD-VENTURE® books you read and they're filled with the same kinds of decisions—but they're longer and have even more ways for the story to end.

So get your older brothers and sisters and anyone else you know between the ages of nine and thirteen in on the fun by introducing them to the exciting world of CHOOSE YOUR OWN ADVENTURE®.

There are over twenty CHOOSE YOUR OWN AD-VENTURE® books for older kids now available wherever Bantam paperbacks are sold.

# WANT TO READ THE MOST EXCITING BOOKS AROUND?
## CHOOSE CHOOSE YOUR OWN ADVENTURE®

Everybody loves CHOOSE YOUR OWN ADVENTURE® books because the stories are about *you*. Each book is loaded with choices that only *you* can make. Instead of reading from the first page to the last page, you read until you come to your first choice. Then, depending on your decision, you turn to a new page to see what happens next. And you can keep reading and rereading CHOOSE YOUR OWN ADVENTURE® books because every choice leads to a new adventure and there are lots of different ways for the story to end.

Buy these great CHOOSE YOUR OWN ADVENTURE® books, available wherever Bantam Skylark books are sold or use the handy coupon below for ordering:

☐ THE HAUNTED HOUSE by R. A. Montgomery (15119-3 * $1.75)
☐ THE CIRCUS by Edward Packard (15120-7 * $1.75)
☐ SUNKEN TREASURE by Edward Packard (15150-9 * $1.75)
☐ SUNKEN TREASURE (Hardcover * 05018-4 * $6.95/$7.95 in Canada)
☐ YOUR VERY OWN ROBOT by R. A. Montgomery (15149-5 * $1.75)
☐ YOUR VERY OWN ROBOT
    (Hardcover * 05019-2 * $6.95/$7.95 in Canada)
☐ GORGA, THE SPACE MONSTER by Edward Packard
    (15161-4 * $1.75)
☐ GORGA, THE SPACE MONSTER
    (Hardcover * 05031-1 * $6.95/$7.95 in Canada)
☐ THE GREEN SLIME by R. A. Montgomery (15162-2 * $1.75)
☐ THE GREEN SLIME (Hardcover * 05032-X * $6.95/$7.95 in Canada)
☐ HELP! YOU'RE SHRINKING by Edward Packard (15195-9 * $1.95)
☐ INDIAN TRAIL by R. A. Montgomery (15201-7 * $1.95)

---

Bantam Books, Inc., Dept. AV5, 414 East Golf Road, Des Plaines, Ill. 60016

Please send me the books I have checked above. I am enclosing $_____
(please add $1.25 to cover postage and handling, send check or money order—no cash or C.O.D.'s please).

Mr/Ms _____

Address _____

City/State _____ Zip _____

AV8—4/83

Please allow four to six weeks for delivery. This offer expires 10/83.

Now you can have your favorite Choose Your Own Adventure® Series in a variety of sizes. Along with the popular pocket size, Bantam has introduced the Choose Your Own Adventure® series in a Skylark edition and also in Hardcover.

Now not only do you get to decide on how you want your adventures to end, you also get to decide on what size you'd like to collect them in.

### SKYLARK EDITIONS

| | | | |
|---|---|---|---|
| ☐ | 15120 | The Circus #1  E. Packard | $1.75 |
| ☐ | 15207 | The Haunted House #2  R. A. Montgomery | $1.95 |
| ☐ | 15208 | Sunken Treasure #3  E. Packard | $1.95 |
| ☐ | 15149 | Your Very Own Robot #4  R. A. Montgomery | $1.75 |
| ☐ | 15308 | Gorga, The Space Monster #5  E. Packard | $1.95 |
| ☐ | 15309 | The Green Slime #6  S. Saunders | $1.95 |
| ☐ | 15195 | Help! You're Shrinking #5  E. Packard | $1.95 |
| ☐ | 15201 | Indian Trail #8  R. A. Montgomery | $1.95 |
| ☐ | 15191 | The Genie In the Bottle #10  J. Razzi | $1.95 |
| ☐ | 15222 | The Big Foot Mystery #11  L. Sonberg | $1.95 |
| ☐ | 15223 | The Creature From Millers Pond #12  S. Saunders | $1.95 |
| ☐ | 15226 | Jungle Safari #13  E. Packard | $1.95 |
| ☐ | 15227 | The Search For Champ #14  S. Gilligan | $1.95 |

### HARDCOVER EDITIONS

| | | | |
|---|---|---|---|
| ☐ | 05018 | Sunken Treasure  E. Packard | $6.95 |
| ☐ | 05019 | Your Very Own Robot  R. A. Montgomery | $6.95 |
| ☐ | 05031 | Gorga, The Space Monster #5  E. Packard | $7.95 |
| ☐ | 05032 | Green Slime #6  S. Saunders | $7.95 |

**Prices and availability subject to change without notice.**

Buy them at your local bookstore or use this handy coupon for ordering: